Guinea Pigs go to Sea

Also by Vivian French

Guinea Pigs on the Go
Morris the Mouse Hunter
Morris in the Apple Tree
Morris and the Cat Flap

Guinea Pigs go to Sea

Vivian French

Illustrated by Clive Scruton

Collins

An imprint of HarperCollins*Publishers*

For Roseanne, with much love

20056205

MORAY COUNCIL
LIBRARIES &
INFORMATION SERVICES
JB

First published in Great Britain by Collins in 2001
Collins is an imprint of HarperCollins*Publishers* Ltd
77-85 Fulham Palace Road, Hammersmith, London W6 8JB

The HarperCollins website address is www.**fire**and**water**.com

1 3 5 7 9 8 6 4 2

Text copyright © Vivian French 2001
Illustrations copyright © Clive Scruton 2001

ISBN 000 675038 9

The author and illustrator assert the moral right to be
identified as the author and illustrator of the work.

Printed and bound in Great Britain by
Omnia Books Limited, Glasgow

Conditions of Sale
This book is sold subject to the condition
that it shall not, by way of trade or otherwise,
be lent, re-sold, hired out or otherwise circulated
without the publisher's prior consent in any form,
binding or cover other than that in which it is
published and without a similar condition
including this condition being imposed on the
subsequent purchaser.

CHAPTER ONE

The sun was hot, and the sea was blue.

Mrs Gussie Guinea Pig was asleep on her blow-up sun bed.

Mille and Tillie and Minnie and Winnie were building the biggest sandcastle in the world.

Snuffler was playing with his new red beach ball.

"OW!" said Millie. "Snuffler threw his ball at me!"

"Didn't," said Snuffler.

"You did," said Tillie. "I saw you!"

"Didn't," said Snuffler.

"DID!" said Minnie and Winnie.

Snuffler began to sniffle.

Mrs Gussie Guinea Pig opened one eye. "Now, my dears," she said. "Be nice to each other!"

"Snuffler's not nice," said Millie. "He threw his ball at me and now my swimming suit's all sandy."

Mrs Gussie Guinea Pig sighed.
It was not easy being the mother of
four children, she thought. Or was it
five? She had never been quite sure.
Mrs Gussie was not good at counting.

"Why don't you all go and have a
paddle?" she said.

"Want to go swimming," said
Snuffler.

Mrs Gussie looked pleased. "WHAT a good idea! Millie and Tillie and Minnie and Winnie will take you for a lovely swim."

"But we don't want to go swimming!" Minnie said. "We're building the biggest sandcastle in the world!"

Mrs Gussie sighed again. "Take Snuffler for a little swim," she said, "and I'll get our picnic ready."

Snuffler jumped up and down. "WINK! WINK! WINK! Have we got lettuce pie? And carrot sandwiches? And potato peelings? And parsnip juice?"

Mrs Gussie smiled fondly. "Yes, dear. I've packed all your favourite things."

"I don't like lettuce pie," said Millie.

"And I don't like carrot sandwiches," said Tillie.

"I HATE potato peelings," said Minnie.

"And I HATE parsnip juice," said Winnie. "Isn't there anything else?"

Mrs Gussie shook her head. "No, dear."

"You're just fusspots," said Snuffler. "Aren't they, Mumsy? They're all fusspots. I eat EVERYTHING! Don't I, Mumsy?"

Mrs Gussie patted Snuffler's head. "SUCH a good, clever boy!" she said proudly.

Minnie and Winnie rolled their eyes.

Millie and Tillie pretended to be sick.

"Now my dears," said Mrs Gussie.
"You run down to the sea while I get
our picnic ready."

"Want to take my beach ball," said Snuffler.

"No, dear," said Mrs Gussie. "It's not safe."

Snuffler clutched his ball tightly and took a deep breath.

"Here he goes," said Minnie.

"Watch out!" said Winnie.

"Cover your ears!" said Millie.

"Cry baby!" said Tillie.

"WANT MY BALL!" yelled Snuffler
at the top of his voice. "WANT IT!
WANT IT! WANT IT! Boo HOO! Boo
HOO! Boo HOO!"

Mrs Gussie made soothing noises.
"There there," she said. "You can take
your ball. Minnie and Winnie will
make sure you're safe. And Millie and
Tillie will help you swim."

Snuffler stopped crying at once.

"Can we go swimming NOW?" he
asked.

"Of course, dear," said Mrs Gussie.
"But put your arm bands on."

Minnie snorted loudly. "He ALWAYS
gets his own way!" she said to Millie.

"He's HORRIBLE!" said Millie to
Tillie.

"He's SPOILT!" said Tillie to Winnie.

Winnie didn't say anything. She was
thinking.

"Come along Snuffler," she said, after a little while. "I'll help you with your arm bands."

Mrs Gussie beamed. Snuffler looked very surprised.

"Winnie!" hissed Minnie. "What are you DOING?"

"Shhh!" whispered Winnie. "I've got an idea."

"You can't have," said Minnie. "It's ME that has ideas!"

"I do too!" said Winnie, and she went on helping Snuffler.

CHAPTER TWO

Mrs Gussie Guinea Pig watched Minnie
and Winnie and Millie and Tillie take
Snuffler down to the edge of the sea.

"What good children I have," she
thought. "Maybe I'll buy them a celery
lolly each. They ALL like celery lollies.
And a packet of turnip crisps. They like
those too."

Mrs Gussie picked up her bag and set
off to the beach shop.

None of her children saw her go. They
were too busy jumping up and down in
the waves.

"Deeper!" said Snuffler. "I want to swim!"

"You can't swim," said Millie.

"You just float about!" said Tillie.

"I CAN swim!" Snuffler told them. "I can! I CAN!"

"Of COURSE you can swim," said
Winnie. "You're a BRILLIANT
swimmer."

Snuffler began to paddle and kick as
hard as he could. He went round and
round in circles.

Millie and Tillie giggled. Winnie
clapped loudly.

Minnie scowled at Winnie. "Go on then," she said. "Tell us your idea."

Winnie splashed closer to Minnie. "I thought if we were nice to Snuffler," she whispered, "he might ask Mother if we can all have celery lollies."

Minnie snorted very loudly indeed. "He NEVER will," she said. "And anyway, I'd rather have turnip crisps."

"YUM!" said Millie.

"Celery lollies are much nicer," said Tillie, and she splashed Millie.

"Ooof!" Millie said, and splashed Tillie back. "They AREN'T nicer!"

"They ARE!" said Winnie, and swooshed water at Minnie.

"TURNIP CRISPS FOR EVER!" said Minnie, and she ducked Winnie.

"CELERY LOLLIES FOR EVER AND EVER AND NO RETURNS!" said Tillie as she ducked Millie.

"HEY!" said Minnie, as Winnie and Millie came up spluttering. "WHERE'S SNUFFLER?"

Winnie and Tillie and Millie stared at her. Then they looked round. There was no sign of Snuffler anywhere.

"Oh NO!" said Tillie. "He's DROWNED!"

"He can't have, Minnie said. "He's got his arm bands on."

"He's probably gone back to Mother," said Winnie.

"LOOK!" said Millie, and she pointed.

They all looked where she was pointing... and there was Snuffler. He was bobbing over the waves holding his new red beach ball tightly... and he was going steadily out to sea.

"SNUFFLER!" yelled Minnie and Winnie.

"COME BACK!" shouted Millie and Tillie.

"I'm swimming... I'm swimming... I'm swimming," Snuffler called back.

"Quick!" said Minnie. "Get Mother!"

Millie and Tillie ran out of the water.
They raced up the sand. There was the
blow-up sun bed. But there was no Mrs
Gussie.

Millie looked at Tillie. Tillie looked at Millie. Then they grabbed the sun bed and rushed back to the sea.

CHAPTER THREE

Minnie and Winnie and Millie and
Tillie climbed on to the sun bed.

"Here we go!" said Minnie.

"Hurrah!" said Millie and Tillie.

"We're coming, Snuffler!" called
Winnie, and she waved.

The sun bed turned over.

Four very wet little guinea pigs
climbed back on again.

"NO MORE WAVING," said Minnie.
"Start paddling!"

Minnie and Winnie and Tillie and
Millie paddled. The sun bed moved
slowly after Snuffler. The waves floated
them up... and the waves floated them
down. Sometimes they could see Snuffler...

and sometimes they couldn't.

"We're not going fast enough," said Minnie. "Paddle harder!"

Minnie and Winnie and Tillie and Millie paddled harder. "Are we getting closer?" asked Tillie.

"I'm not sure," said Minnie.
"I think so," said Millie.
"I'm getting tired," said Winnie.
They paddled grimly on.
"Can you see him?" asked Minnie.
"No," said Millie and Tillie.

"Snuffler!" called Winnie. "Are you all right?"

"Coo-ee!" Snuffler called back. "Guess what I can see!"

"Seaweed?" said Minnie.

"Seagulls?" said Millie.

"Waves?" said Tillie.

"Starfish?" said Winnie.

"Silly billies!" called Snuffler. "It's a shark!"

"EEEEEEEEK!" shrieked his sisters.

"Don't talk to it!" screamed Millie and Tillie.

"Don't touch it!" yelled Winnie and Minnie.

They paddled harder than ever, puffing and panting.

A wave heaved the sun bed up... and then down again.

"Ooooh!" said Winnie. "I feel sick!"

"Who cares?" puffed Minnie, rudely. "Snuffler, can you hear me?"

"Yes!" Snuffler sounded very cheerful. "Come and see Sharkie!"

Millie burst into tears. "He's going to
be eaten!" she wailed.

Tillie began to cry too. "And we were
so horrid to him!"

"DEAR little Snuffler!" sniffled
Winnie.

"Be quiet and keep paddling!"
snapped Minnie.

Another wave heaved them up in the air... and they saw Snuffler clearly.

He was patting a fish. A very large fish. A fish with a long sharp nose. A fish with a VERY long sharp nose...

"THAT'S NOT A SHARK!" shouted
Minnie. "THAT'S A SWORDFISH!"

The swordfish looked round. It saw
the sun bed on the top of the wave.

It saw four heads peering down. It saw four wide open mouths. It saw eight paws waving.

"AAAGH!" gasped the swordfish, "A SEA MONSTER!" And it dived...

...and as it dived it sliced a hole in
Snuffler's new red beach ball.

HISSSSSSSSSSSSSSSS!!!

Bubbles burst out in a long stream...

...and Snuffler and the beach ball
zoomed over the waves towards the
shore.

CHAPTER FOUR

Minnie and Winnie and Millie and
Tillie stared and stared and stared.

"He's FLYING!" said Millie and Tillie.
"He's FLYING over the sea!"

"He's THERE!" said Minnie and
Winnie. "He's THERE on the shore!"
They were right.

Snuffler and his beach ball hit the
beach and flopped on to the sand.

"He's getting up," said Minnie.

"He's picking up his ball," said

Winnie.

"What's left of it," said Millie.

"He's looking at it," said Tillie.

"Now he's sitting down again," said Minnie.

"Bet he's howling," said Winnie.

"He is," said Millie and Tillie.

"QUICK!" said Minnie. "We've GOT to get back before Mother sees him on his own."

"But I'm SO tired," moaned Winnie.

"Us too," groaned Millie and Tillie.

Minnie looked at her sisters. Then she looked at the sun bed. "AHA!" she said. "I've had an idea!"

"Is it a good one?" asked Millie.

"Not like Winnie's idea," said Tillie.

"It wasn't my fault it went wrong!" said Winnie.

"This," said Minnie, "is my best idea ever." And she pulled the plug out of the sun bed.

"NOOOOOOOOOOOOOO!"
screamed Winnie and Millie and
Tillie... but the sun bed was already
blowing bubbles.

"Here we go!" yelled Minnie, as the sun bed raced away towards the beach... and landed just in front of Snuffler.

"Boo HOO! Boo HOO! Boo – er?" said Snuffler, as Minnie and Winnie and Millie and Tillie rolled on to the sand. The sun bed gave one last final SSSsssss and went totally flat.

Minnie jumped up first. She shaded her eyes and peered up the beach. There was Mrs Gussie – just walking towards their sunshade and towels.

"QUICK!" hissed Minnie. "Millie and Tillie – GET BLOWING!"

Millie and Tillie took it in turns to blow up the sun bed. When they were puffed out Minnie and Winnie took over.

"I want a go!" demanded Snuffler.

"Ooooomp ooomp ooomp OOOMP,"
said Minnie, blowing hard.

"She means NO WAY," said Winnie.

"WANT TO BLOW!" shouted Snuffler.

"You can have a go later," said Millie.

"I think it's blown up enough now," said Tillie.

Minnie pushed in the plug. "HURRY!" she hissed.

Winnie grabbed Snuffler's paw. "Come along, Snuffler," she said. "Time for a lovely picnic."

CHAPTER FIVE

Mrs Gussie Guinea Pig smiled happily.
She could see all her children (was it
five? or was it four? She did WISH she
could remember). There they were,
sitting nicely on the sun bed, drying
little Snuffler's fur.

Mrs Gussie felt very pleased that she had walked to the shop to buy her children a treat... a much nicer treat than celery lollies or turnip crisps.

"Here I am, my dears," she said. "And I've got a LOVELY surprise for you after you've eaten your food!"

"Thank you, Mother," said Minnie and Winnie and Millie and Tillie.

Mrs Gussie wondered why the four (or was it five?) girls looked rather tired. Perhaps it was too hot for them?

She patted Snuffler's head. "It's a treat for you too, dear," she said.

"MUMSY," squeaked Snuffler. "I went for a ride on my new beach ball and I seed a shark and I patted it and it made a hole in my ball and I ZOOMED back faster than a ROCKET!"

"Oh, Snuffler, dear," said Mrs Gussie. "What a CLEVER story! But guess what? After you've eaten up your lettuce pie and carrot sandwiches and potato peelings, we're ALL going to go in a boat. We're going to paddle our very own boat all the way out to sea!"

"HURRAH!" said Snuffler. "I LOVE paddling!"

Minnie and Winnie and Millie and Tillie didn't say anything. They were fast asleep and snoring on the blow-up sun bed.